AF439647

THE
CHRISTMAS DRAGON

AMONG THE MYTHOS BOOK 1

RUTHANNE REID

CONTENTS

Copyright © 2014 by **Ruthanne Reid**

All rights reserved. No part of this publication may be reproduced, distributed or transmitted in any form or by any means, without prior written permission.

NO AI TRAINING: Without in any way limiting the author's exclusive rights under copyright, any use of this publication to "train" generative artificial intelligence (AI) technologies to generate text is expressly prohibited. The author reserves all rights to license uses of this work for generative AI training and development of machine learning language models.

www.ruthannereid.com

Publisher's Note: This is a work of fiction. Names, characters, places, and incidents are a product of the author's imagination. Locales and public names are sometimes used for atmospheric purposes. Any resemblance to actual people, living or dead, or to businesses, companies, events, institutions, or locales is completely coincidental.

The Christmas Dragon/ Ruthanne Reid. – 1st ed.

✶ HUMAN AUTHORED

Reg #: 8899248, https://authorsguild.org/human

*Duane, you believe I can write even when I can only see my errors.
You are, as always, the best.*

"One way to stop a runaway horse is to bet on him."

——Jeffrey Bernard

CHAPTER 1

THE BOX

The box jumped.

Boxes are not supposed to jump. It's a law somewhere, I think. Maybe Guyana. Apparently not in New Hampshire, because the box kept jumping.

I sat in my idling car, puffs of exhaust rising in my rearview mirror, and stared at the uncoordinated box-dance. Said box was wrapped in the loveliest paper, too, which was a shame, because bouncing on my boot scraper had roughened all the corners and torn one edge. The bow was big and purple and covered in small green somethings. I wasn't close enough to make them out.

I didn't want to be close enough to make them out.

If I didn't do something soon, the neighbors would notice. The box probably hadn't been jumping all morning, or there'd be a crowd. Or maybe it was already on YouTube. I didn't know.

So much for a safe, boring life among the Ever-Dying. New Hampshire, you have failed me.

I turned off the car. Time to go see what invaded my (mostly) magic-free space.

I did have a little magic, though admittedly I hadn't used it in three years except to fix my hair on the go, so let's just say I found myself rusty. Myself, and my wand. It was a little rusty. No, for real. Real wands are made of iron, didn't you know? Better conductors.

So there I was in my New England suburb, staring into my trunk at my rusted wand while a box jumped on my front porch, and I will admit I wanted to run away. This situation was so bizarre that I couldn't help wondering if (a) my family sent it, or (b) this was some kind of horrible, evil trap. Both options were silly on consideration. With one exception, my family doesn't know where I am, and for another thing, I am absolutely and completely not worth some bad guy's time. I didn't even graduate college, for crying out loud.

The box kept jumping. It might have growled. I sighed, took my wand from the trunk, and hid it in my long winter coat for the treacherous walk to the front porch.

This time of year, ice covers everything. You'd think that this far north it would be the snow that gets you, but nope—it's the ice. Ice on top of snow, layered with more snow, and finally more ice to top off this slippery sundae. Even my kick-ass boots only gave me so much traction, and I had to sort of inch my way along the walk.

My neighbor's teenage son chose that moment to push the snowblower out of his garage.

Almost there. Inch, inch, inch—

"Hey, Katie," Kyle called from across the street, and I waved at him and prayed he wouldn't notice anything amiss. "Want me to dig your mailbox out?" he said.

The snowplows had buried it. As usual. "Thanks, sure. And tell your mom I owe her a coffee for last week," I said, pouring all my focus into appearing friendly and nice and normal. My footing slipped. I caught myself, arms out for balance, bent over like a really bad skier.

The box jumped again. Dammit, box, I was almost there.

"What's that?" Kyle said.

"Mexican jumping beans!" I announced because I watch too many cartoons. And then I fell.

I managed to grab the porch railing to prevent breaking my ass on the ice, but this was not ideal because Kyle was a good kid. He was halfway across the cul-de-sac before I had the chance to right myself.

"I'm okay!" I called, hanging off the banister with one bemittened hand and holding up the other in the international sign for *stop right there, buster.* "I'm good! I'm *all right!*" My boot heels squeaked on the ice as I fought for footing.

Kyle stopped, but he looked fairly alarmed, and that meant it was time to go. Arm aching, face red, I grabbed the box and threw myself inside.

Two things occurred here that shouldn't have: one, the door unlocked and opened all by itself, though I hadn't even touched it. Two, I realized the box was hot. Really hot. I dropped it.

It squeaked. The jumping box squeaked.

Great. Something was alive in there, and since my lock wasn't broken and my wards weren't tripped, whatever it was, it generated enough magic to overwhelm mine and snap it like stretched gum.

I picked up the box again, hoping I hadn't killed whatever was in there. Though maybe killing it was smart, before it got out and did what it was here to do.

No, I didn't have the stomach for that. I couldn't kill some helpless thing in a box. Seriously? You'd have to be a monster to do that without hesitation.

It wasn't jumping anymore when I put it down on the counter, though it was still really hot. I tapped the top.

Something in there scratched back, trying to get out.

Screw this. I wasn't wasting my evening playing guess-the-content with this thing. I had a date (finally), and my decidedly normal coworker would not understand a jumping, squeaking box that might contain something demonic.

So I pointed my wand and opened it.

Kin magic has no fanfare. Most magic is really showy (usually produced by Fey and other weirdos), but Kin magic just happens. It's like flipping a switch. Trumpets don't play when the bathroom fan comes on, either.

The box blew apart, double-thick cardboard smacking to the counter. Inside sat a tiny, perfect, snow-white dragon.

A dragon. On my kitchen counter. It squeaked at me, which could mean absolutely anything, and began to preen itself like a cat.

I may have grown up in the magical world, but even there, dragons aren't common. They're nearly extinct; the eastern Elders hid themselves in the earth somewhere long ago, and the western Red and Black clans are quite occupied with wiping each other out. In fact, dragons were declared endangered sometime in the sixteenth century—yet here a baby one stood, chewing clumsily at its dark claws.

Mother-of-pearl scales gleamed all over its ridiculously long, thin neck. The wee round-bellied body rested on tiny curved legs and a tail long enough to balance that neck. Its head was a drawn-out diamond, long and narrow, and its snout was so thin that the flare of its nostrils only emphasized the disproportionate cuteness of the whole package.

I'd never seen anything so adorable in my life.

Without warning, he chirped at me and jumped off the counter.

I caught him just before he hit the floor. He felt fragile like a frog—warm and soft with loose, smooth skin over teeny tiny bones. I stroked his sides and his tiny little legs, winced at the sharpness of his adorable little claws, and discovered an outline of wings hidden under the skin of his ridged back.

He looked at me warmly, leaned into my touch, and then puked fire all over my boots.

It wasn't controlled. There was no distance achieved, just a messy splash of liquid flame straight down. I whooped and danced backward, throwing magic in a mad attempt to prevent my toes melting, or the floor melting, since this was a rental and I wanted my security deposit back.

I was glad Kyle couldn't hear all this. I'm pretty sure I said a few curse words he'd never heard before.

The little dragon clung to my hand, claws digging in for dear life. He looked as spooked as I was by what had happened.

"The hell did you do that for?" I said, carrying him to the sink.

He didn't want to let go of my hand. Too bad. Even cute things need washing.

"Hey," I said to him as he wriggled and protested under the hot water. "Hey. Stop being cute. I mean it. I can't keep you."

Of course, he didn't heed.

"Okay, Katie," I told myself as I rubbed his soft underbelly. "You've always wanted a dragon friend. Look how cute he is, just hatched and already barfing fire!" He'd left some black burned spots on the linoleum, which I had no idea how to fix, or how to explain to my landlord.

Yeah, this wouldn't end well. I couldn't keep the little guy.

Which led to a problem. It wasn't like I could set him loose. I was also pretty sure both the local ASPCA and orphanages would find themselves ill-equipped, because he was not an animal, and was too young to have a human form.

The microwave blinked 6:52, which meant it was 4:30 (I'd never reset it after the last power outage). I had an hour before this evening's date was scheduled to appear.

The baby dragon trilled in my hands, a guilelessly happy sound, and wriggled to get his tiny face under the water.

I was unregistered. If I went to the local magical authorities for help, they'd know I was here. If I left the poor baby on their doorstep, who knew what they'd do to him? He was unregistered, too, and unlike me, didn't have the wherewithal to defend himself.

I couldn't keep him. I couldn't get help here. I knew only one way to safely guarantee he'd be okay: I'd have to call my family.

Dammit, dammit, dammit. This was not how Katie Lin rolled. When I'd left them for a normal life, I'd meant it, and when I said I'd never talk to them again, it was a solemn vow. They didn't even know I was dating. Or had dropped out of college. Or lived in the sticks.

Generational war has its casualties, and not all family loss is due to death. No, there had to be another way.

There was: I could take him to my uncle. I trusted my uncle. He even had my address. Maybe this could work.

Evidently, I had previously unknown skill in dragon wrangling. The baby dragon trilled constantly, like a purr, and pressed into my fingers. At least I wouldn't give him a name. Nope. I absolutely would not, because I wasn't keeping him, and Vesuvius wouldn't care what I called him anyway.

Well, dammit.

I had no choice. It was time for the most epic way to blow off a first date via boring voicemail *ever*. "Hey, Darrin, it's Katie. I—" Vesuvius puked fire again, fortunately into the sink, but it hit the sponge, and the sponge melted. I didn't know they could do that. "Uh. Sorry, dropped something. I hate to do this, but I need to cancel tonight. Sorry this is so abrupt. I'll call you later, okay? Bye."

It's okay. I hadn't really liked him that much, anyway. I just wanted a normal date.

Normal. No food that changes colors or magic singing tablecloths. Normal.

I told myself this. I had to, every day. And that meant I couldn't be the magical one on a date, either, or the Mythos—the magical beings of this world—would get pissed because I'd revealed the truth to the Ever-Dying.

They called my kind Kin, which meant part Ever-Dying (such a flattering word for *human*, isn't it?) and part something else. Technically, I'm about as human as the next guy (I can give blood and everything), but there's just enough *other* in my family tree to extend my lifespan and give me access to magic.

I know someday my attempt to live like a pure-blood human, to love one and spend my life with one (whoever *that* may be), is going to crash and burn in my face, but that day is not today. Today I will keep lying, for as long as it takes, to preserve this fragile and ever-dying life.

Out of curiosity, I checked flights to Wales, but the tickets were out of my price range. I don't really know what I was thinking, anyway. How do you smuggle a baby dragon through customs? Never mind that wands tend to upset the TSA *a lot*. Something about traveling with a giant metal stick bothers them, for some mysterious reason.

I could go by ship, which is how I got to America in the first place, but I doubted that kind of time was available to me. I knew how huge dragons got, but I didn't know how fast they got there. What did he even eat? I didn't know.

That left magical transport. That meant hiding Vesuvius, because I wouldn't risk him being taken away, but without x-ray machines, it might actually be possible.

I put Suvi (Suvi! Even his nickname was cute) in my black oval roasting pan and set him on my bed. He peered sideways over the edge to watch me, resting his tiny cheekbone on the rim.

Clothes: no formal robes, because this was not a "real" visit. I planned to show up at my uncle's door, give him the baby, and leave. If anybody else related to me was there, too bad for them. I didn't want my family to think I was thriving without them—they might react to that—so I settled for a really comfy jogging suit, all plush on the inside and a glorious purple color that made me feel better for no reason at all.

Shoes: practical. Not the boots, because while they were really sturdy, they were useless to run in, and I might need to run. Also, those boots were expensive. Plain old tennis shoes, it was.

Underthings: nobody's business.

Winter coat: the men's coat I used for snow shoveling. Dark green and stained with salt residue, it hung to my knees in a perfect manifestation of *leave me alone, I am not worth your time.*

The rest: my wand, three books for boredom, and a baby dragon nest. I had enough skill to transform a beach towel into something round and squishy and self-heating and soft, and I did my best to make it fire-resistant. Just in case, I threw in a ward to let me know if Vesuvius puked.

I had a sandwich and gave the dragon water in a quarter-cup measure, which he lapped up with his tiny forked tongue. He wouldn't eat. He had no interest in anything in my fridge, meat or otherwise, though he did chew the spinach thoughtfully before spitting it out in squeaking complaint. Well, I'd just have to travel with a hungry baby dragon, then. Hopefully that didn't mean he'd eat my books.

Now there was nothing else delaying me beyond raw, unfiltered cowardice.

I hadn't seen anyone among the Mythos in three years. I'd gone off the grid completely. My failed scholastic career and my current job were sad, but I was proud of them. Success or failure, they were normal. Ordinary. Unmagical. And all of it could go up in smoke if this went wrong.

"Are you worth it, little guy?" I whispered to the warm, soft bundle of scales in my hands, and I kissed him. He chirped and bonked his tiny head against my chin.

Yeah, he was, and I was committed. I put him in his new little home, zipped the bag, and headed out the door.

Those with magic in their blood always know where a conflux is. It pulls us, even the "us" who don't know they're not purely human. Have you ever been pulled in a direction for no reason you could understand, or even felt better just facing that way? Maybe you had time to wander that way for a while, following some wordless urge, only to find nothing to explain your desire. You were probably being called to a conflux. I'm sorry you didn't find it. They're a hell of a thing.

From the outside, they're usually innocuous—a shed, or a nasty-looking bus stop nobody would want to stand in, or an outhouse that some construction company evidently left behind. It's carefully warded; no one among the Ever-Dying wants to go near these things, not even for something illegal.

My nearest conflux looked like a funky little hunting shed, long abandoned, with the door missing and animal droppings everywhere. I ducked inside, stepping carefully (the dung was real), and tapped my wand tip against the floor.

Like an old-fashioned turntable, the cabin started to spin.

The cabin, not me. Undisturbed, I tucked my wand back in my bag as the cabin picked up speed, whirling faster and faster until everything blurred. Right at that moment, lights blazed into existence. The spinning walls and ceiling smoothly pulled away, expanding, brightening, granting ever-slowing glimpses of fancy molding and marble columns.

People (human-looking and otherwise) walked the suddenly-marbled floors as if they weren't wildly spinning around me, and vertigo briefly stole my balance. I closed my eyes, waiting for it to slow down, and when I opened them again, I'd arrived. Warmth and happy seasonal smells greeted me, with hints of pine and cinnamon and something that might have been cranberry. Light marble columns and walls kept it feeling open and airy, regardless of the crowd and the complete lack of windows or doors. Booths built into the distant walls boasted gold scrolling along their eaves and sales reps who managed to look like they wanted to be here.

In spite of all this, the lines were horrifying, stretching all the way to where I stood at the point of arrival, and even with magic, nothing was moving very fast. Dang. Holiday travel sucks, no matter where you go.

I took the line going east.

Sure, with magic it was possible to just go bouncing from country to country, but there isn't a government in the world that likes unwanted visitors. Given the current tension between the Seven Peoples of the Earth, confluxes were the wisest way to go. I'd pay my money, receive a neat little stamp, and arrive in Wales without political ripples.

In front of me stood a trio of ogres. Their suits fit them pretty well, considering the shape and size changes ogres go through on a weekly basis, so they must be ogres with money. I kept my head down (which in this case meant around their elbows) and my hand on my bag. Did baby dragons have a smell? None I could detect, but that didn't mean somebody here couldn't smell it.

Behind me queued a tall Fey fellow, as lovely as they all were, and oh, he knew it. He wore his fitted black peacoat over a white shirt and jeans, emphasizing the admittedly interesting ratio between his shoulders and waist. His hair lay like spun silk over his wide lapels, and his black buckled boots added enough of an edge to keep him from being boring.

That coat had loops on the shoulders. It was double-breasted. I would wear the dickens out of that coat.

He smirked at me.

Envying his coat had led to bad things. Too late, I turned away.

"Hello, there," he said.

I didn't have time for amorous Fey. I opted for ignoring him completely.

Which was a mistake. Fey only grow more obnoxious when ignored. "I don't see many Kin in this area," he said, all smooth and resonant.

For crying out loud . . . "Leave me alone, please."

Fey have pretty laughter, of course. Everything they have is pretty, but I don't like people who get everything so easily in life. Not that I'm jealous. Because I'm not.

So anyway, he laughed. "My apologies. I'll do that, but . . . well, I hope you aren't in a great hurry today."

I stepped closer to the ogres. "As a matter of fact, I am."

"That's too bad. They're closing soon."

I scowled at the distant booths. "Nonsense. Why would they be closing?"

"Thirty minutes to close," came over the loudspeakers. "Thirty minutes! Buy your tickets now, or don't buy 'em at all!"

I just stared at the speakers. Let me tell you something about magical business: when they say something like *thirty minutes, and no more tickets,* they mean it. I was boned.

"Construction," said the Fey fellow cheerfully. "They're refitting this whole conflux to handle all the new traffic, which of course is to be expected."

New traffic to be expected? Why? This was the worst timing possible. I'd have to drive into Boston, or something. Fifteen-dollars-an-hour parking, huzzah. I groaned. My line didn't move, so I left my place and jogged in a wide circle.

No lines were moving. Everything was packed. Everybody else in the room looked upset, and that didn't help me at all. "Dammit!"

"I kept your place," the Fey man said helpfully, and gestured at my former spot with a delicate sweep and an eyebrow wriggle.

I was torn between laughing at him and burning his eyebrows off. Correction: dreaming about burning his eyebrows off, because a fire-mage, I was not. "Thanks," I said, and stepped back in. Guilt niggled. "Sorry I was rude."

He leaned around my side and beamed at me. "No problem."

No problem, he says. Not *you're welcome*, or *my pleasure.* This guy's been stateside for a while.

We stood in slightly less frosty silence for a whole three minutes.

"So what happens if you don't manage to get a ticket?" he said, peeking at my profile. His gaze tracked appreciatively over my straight black hair and my slanted black eyes.

I kept those eyes straight ahead. "Nothing."

"Are you sure?" he said, ignoring my obvious clue when to shut up. "Given the Hunt's presence, it seems a little risky to stay here."

I snorted. "The Hunt isn't around. This isn't their season."

"That doesn't matter." His eyes lidded, and he stood back out of sight again. "They were actually hired, didn't you hear? Something of great value was stolen, and they're hunting to get it back."

Okay, *that* was different, and of course I hadn't heard, because I hadn't been listening at all. This was big. This was bad. "What was stolen?"

"Oh, something small. The Hunt has traced it to this area, which, of course, is why everyone's leaving." He gestured gracefully at the room. "We won't make it to the counter in time. I have another option for you, if you're interested in taking it."

I barely heard what he said because I was busy freaking out.

This was about Vesuvius. I knew it. Why hadn't I stopped to question where this baby came from? Had his egg been in a some treasury, somewhere? The Wild Hunt was unpredictable at the best of times, and I had a baby dragon in my bag. A baby dragon with enough power to pop minor wards and probably set off magical alarms. They would find me.

"Oh," I said, which was lame, but I didn't know what else to say without implicating myself. I should probably watch more lawyer shows.

"Oh?" he repeated, peering around my side again. "Is that a yes?"

"Is what a yes?" I said, trying to remember what he'd offered.

He opened his mouth, but before he could speak, the earth shook.

There's a distinct rhythm to footstep tremors. Even when they're enormously spaced apart, you know, *know,* that something is coming, and all the buzz of conversation stilled as everybody looked around.

The floor shook again, rattling the tiny fairies inside their glass lampshades, and their panicked squeaking crawled up my spine and made the overwhelming silence creepier. Another step, louder, shook plaster dust down on our heads.

"To hell with this," announced the ogre in front of me, but whatever he was going to do, he ran out of time.

The pressure changed so suddenly it felt like ice picks in my ears. I staggered, gasped, and looked up to see mind-blowingly huge hands appear out of nowhere and rip a hole in the air.

Foreign and inimical atmosphere poured into the station, and far away, the sound of hooves rang on something hollow and unforgiving. Unmistakable, unthinkable, inescapable: the Hunt. It was the Wild Hunt, pushing before it a wave of mindless terror because it enjoyed the chase.

Everybody freaked.

In that jagged hole crouched a darkness so deep that it made my eyes ache and water, even though it was hard to look away. Beings large and small stampeded in all directions, and I cried out as the ogres knocked me over in their haste to get away. There was nowhere to *go.* No doors or windows, just one spinning exit blocked by that tear which no one was going near because *really,* and yes, the no-exits policy seems unwise, but magical people are just arrogant like that. There aren't many things out there that could tear the magical protections of a conflux. The Hunt had brought big, bad help to rip into our dimension.

Just then, the Fey ducked low and ran. He didn't look panicked. He scuttled with purpose. Where the hell was he going? I followed.

Fey are devilish slippery things, but I managed to keep up in the chaos.

Everyone shouted and ran around, waving weapons or cowering behind puny magical shields. I weaved between large hairy bodies and bounced off leathery, brick-hard ones, reflecting that I hadn't been in a situation like this in ages, and boy, I had not missed it.

I was so tiny compared to most of the things in here. A blue-furred gorgad knocked me down, and when I looked up, the damned Fey was gone.

Some idiot cast a fog spell, and now no one could see anything. I crawled one-handed through the screams, awkward, clutching the bag to my chest and praying Vesuvius hadn't been smothered or smushed or worse. I didn't dare stand. Wet, ripping sounds filtered through the screams and spell casting. I panted and moved forward, trying to reach the wall.

The fog was lighter there, and I spotted him again: the Fey, fiddling with an item I couldn't quite see.

This dude had a way out. I didn't bother shouting. I just jumped to my feet and ran at him.

He saw me coming, and his face flickered through annoyance, surprise, and then welcome as he gestured at me to hurry.

He had a portal. It gleamed at his feet—a small, silver disc the size of a dollar coin, emitting light in thick white rays like the beams from a cartoon sun. In the middle of this chaos, the Fey bowed and gestured me toward it with all the grace of an old-world gentleman, and I revamped my original theory: he may have been in the States for a while, but he definitely started out somewhere else.

I leaped into the rays without bothering to ask where we were going. Whoever said I can't be spontaneous?

CHAPTER 2

THE STARLING

No one expects the Spanish Inquisition!

Sorry about that. It should actually read: no one expects the desert, and Fey portals that dump you into one while you're wearing full winter clothing are kind of a surprise, too.

I hadn't been in a Fey portal in years, and I nearly broke my neck. Traveling through one is like stepping on an icy path with just enough of an incline to get you moving. You don't really have any control. All you can do is crouch, keep your balance, and hope you don't smash into anything on the other side.

I was not prepared for sand. I stumbled, twisting so that as I went down (which was *at once*), I wouldn't crush my bag and its precious cargo.

The Fey fellow alighted behind me as daintily as you please, pausing to brush plaster dust off his sleeves before closing the portal. He collected all that power as if gently gathering a spiderweb, tucked it away in his pocket, and only then looked at me, sprawled on the sand. His expression was not nice. "What are you carrying?"

I had sand in my underwear. I was in trouble, big trouble, and I had sand in my underwear. "One ring to rule them all?"

He raised his eyebrows. "Try again. Carrying you through was ridiculously difficult, and I know no Kin with that much magic. What are you carrying with you?"

Well, *I* knew Kin with that much magic. My uncle qualified, but this guy didn't need to know that. "A gift for my uncle. I don't think you need to know what it is."

He looked around. "Oh? So you have another way out of here?"

Jerk. "Are you seriously threatening to leave me here?"

"I'm not even sure I can get us both out," he snapped. "What, did you think I aimed for the Simpson Desert?"

I looked blank.

"Australia!" he said. "We're in the Outback!"

"So that's why it's so hot," I said, because I was already sweating through my layers. The sand was so red, almost blindingly bright. Maybe it had a sunburn. Sandburn?

He pinched the bridge of his nose, and his ears flicked back. Fey share that trait with cats: ears go back, irritation on the rise. "One more time, or I swear to the moon I'm leaving you here: What are you carrying with you?"

I'm not good at lying. The real issue, though, was the fact that I didn't know if he'd really leave me there, and I didn't have enough magic to get out of there on my own. The baby dragon still hadn't eaten anything, either. "Mind giving me a hand up before the interrogation? Among the Mythos, I'm Kin, called Katie."

Banking on his old-world manners worked. He scowled but pulled me to my feet. "Among the Mythos, I'm Unseelie Fey. Called Grey." His eyes narrowed, and then he began to circle me, magically checking me out. "You're unusual."

"Yes. I am unusually hot," I said, unzipping my jacket.

He gave me a once-over. "Mm-hm. But you know that isn't what I meant."

Did he really just hit on me now? Now? "Would it kill you to get us out of here before we play twenty questions, Romeo?"

"It might, unless I know what I'm carrying so I can compensate for it." He leaned in. His eyes were almost silver, that unique-to-Fey gray with thin black lines radiating out from his pupils. I might have gotten lost in them, just a little. He might have intended me to, just a little. "Answer my question."

Willpower washed over me. He was strong. Really strong. I was going to lose if I played this game. "Grey, I'm not your enemy. I just need a little help getting to Wales, and my uncle can make it worth your time, I swear."

"Your uncle?"

I nodded. "He's wealthy, generous, and really nice. He'll make it up to you. I promise."

He sighed and stood back, arms crossed. "Say it one more time, and we have a deal."

I swallowed. An oath said three times is binding, and I was guaranteeing someone else's behavior. But my uncle had never let me down before. I had to believe he'd make good. "I swear. You'll be reimbursed in full."

Grey pulled the coin out of his pocket. "Where in Wales?"

Yay, avarice! I wasn't going to be stuck in the desert. Relief stole my intelligence, and I told him the truth. "Bardsey Island."

He stared at me.

I stared back. In two stupid words, I'd told him far more than he needed to know.

"You're a Lin," he said, and took a step back.

Oh, this would not end well. "Technically."

"I am *not* helping a Lin!" He took another step.

I couldn't blame him, and I couldn't chase him, or he might freak out and do who knew what. "I know what you're thinking, but I'm not like them! Why do you think I'm living in freaking New Hampshire?" I raised my hands as if asking for arrest. "Please, don't leave me here!"

He stopped retreating, but now he bared his teeth. "And your uncle? You think I don't know who lives on that island?"

Caught.

He'd never help me now. The Fey hated the Lins and were terrified of my uncle. The Lins were important people. Wealthy. Powerful. Austere. They protected themselves and their interests. Guess what? The Fey do the same thing. The conflicts over land, magical items, and inheritance from mixed-species offspring were endless.

Ah, but then there's my uncle.

My last name is Lin. As in *Merlin*.

Merlin: a silly name my uncle Myrddin adopted because he has a sense of humor, and he's culturally astute. He's not like the rest of my family, and I'm not like them, either, but my uncle has the power to fight back when pressure is applied. I don't, which is why I ran. I closed my eyes and rode a wave of old but unforgotten shame, the reminder of why I'd fled.

I was genuinely surprised to find Grey still there when I looked up again. "You didn't go?"

He hadn't come any closer, either. "Do you want me to? What are you carrying, Miss Lin? I'll take that knowledge as a down payment."

He might *not* leave me here. This guy had a spine. "Please just call me Katie. And you know what? I'd better show you. You'd never believe me otherwise." I put the bag on the ground, prayed its wee occupant was not dead, and unzipped the top.

Suvi popped out like bread from a broken toaster and landed on the sand, white on red like a tooth in a strange, gaping smile. Proud of himself, he stomped with teeny-tiny menace, leaving little divots about the size of the blunt end of a pencil.

He was so cute I just about died.

Grey's mouth hung open. He looked like he'd never blink again. "That's a dragon."

"Isn't he adorbs?" I knelt and scooped him up, deeply grateful he hadn't puked fire everywhere. Vesuvius roared, or tried, and attempted to keep stomping in my hand. In other words, he wriggled a lot.

"That's a dragon," Grey said again.

"You noticed?" I raised my eyebrow in a display of perfect irony, which was wasted because Grey wasn't looking at me.

"He's white. He's white! Shit!" Grey gripped his hair in both hands and paced in a wild circle, like he had to go somewhere, but didn't know which way to run. "Holy shit, he's white!"

I rubbed the top of Suvi's wee head with one fingertip. "Okay. Obviously, this means something I don't know. Are you going to fill me in?"

He'd gone as pale as his platinum hair. "The Hunt is looking for a *star-hued child with a heart of fire.*"

Well, there was my confirmation. Doom-hunches for the win. A moment of silent horribleness passed between us. The Hunt wanted the baby dragon. The baby dragon was with me. Grey had just helped me escape them. He was probably going to be targeted. "My uncle can keep us safe from the Hunt."

Grey spun and stared at me. "He can?"

"He can."

Grey's color now matched his name. "And he won't . . . he won't do anything to me?"

And that's how terrible my uncle's reputation is. "I swear, he won't. You come as my friend, he'll treat you that way."

His color did not improve, but he finally believed me. "We have to get out of here. Now." He threw the coin to the sand, and its rays cut through the clear desert air with squint-worthy brilliance.

I cuddled Suvi (in spite of annoyed wriggles) and tucked him back in my bag. "We're almost home, baby."

"In. In, in, in!" Grey gestured, and I jumped.

The sudden change from what had to be over a hundred degrees Fahrenheit to something closer to forty briefly stole my breath. It was two in the morning on Bardsey Island, and there were no cities to add light or sound. Darkness, peace, and the distant sound of ocean-on-shore wrapped around me like familiar arms.

This place with its ancient dreams, its beauty and serenity, made it hard not to miss everything I'd left behind. Just for a moment, anyway, I missed the magic, the ease, the joy of living with color and power. Light from the lone lighthouse failed to dim the stars. I just breathed, gathering strength, and stared up at the vast, cold quiet of space.

"Where?" Grey's ears trembled.

I almost pitied him. "Grey, calm down. We're fine."

"I doubt that," he said expansively, and stared around with wide, horse-crazy eyes.

"Dude. Seriously. Chill." Hearing myself say these ridiculously American words while standing on distinctly non-American soil made me giggle, and Grey looked at me like I was the craziest thing he'd ever seen. I reined it in for his sake. "My uncle won't harm you."

"You can't know that."

I started up the hill. "Actually, I can. My uncle *wants* everybody to think he's some kind of dangerous psycho. It keeps visitors away."

"Ha!" he said, as though I made no sense, but he followed me anyway.

The island was only about a mile long. Minimal light pollution made silhouettes of the Celtic crosses and ruined thirteenth-century abbey, beneath which twenty thousand saints supposedly lay buried.

There was no structure at the top of the island's single hill—at least, nothing the Ever-Dying could see. Near it is a tiny cave, which the Ever-Dying think is the resting place of Merlin the Magician. Myrddin, however, has no interest in hiding in a cave, and you can pronounce it *mur-thin,* thank you very much.

My uncle is old, very old, an age only some among the Mythos can reach. Sometimes he looks young, and sometimes he doesn't, and there seems to be no rhyme or reason why. He was already old when the real King Arthur did what he could to defend his home against invaders, and in my uncle's mind, the real King Arthur was also the greatest man history ever produced.

Arthur isn't dead, for the record. He was *dying.* My uncle put him in some kind of stasis, looking forward to such a time as he could bring this poor Ever-Dying king back and keep him alive for good. Why? To rule the world, I guess. Or maybe just Wales. Seriously, I don't know, but my uncle acts like this Arthur will solve all the world's problems.

Well, as of yet, there's no way to keep the Ever-Dying alive forever, so Arthur stays snoozing—but none of that explains why Grey was scared.

You know about the Romans and the Anglo-Saxons, about the Vikings and the Danes and the Scottish and the Picts. There have been a lot of wars here to control these islands, but I wager you don't know about the Seelie and Unseelie courts. Around a thousand years ago, during the last big push for blood purity, the courts of the Seelie and Unseelie Fey actually managed to agree on something: Kin were vermin. Determined to cleanse the land, they banded together and stormed the Norman city of London.

My uncle fought back.

They'd forgotten he was here. Everybody had forgotten he was here, except the Ever-Dying, and who listens to them? When the courts came at London in the first wave of magic and death, my uncle rose from the shadows like a mother bear and blew their armies away. He batted aside the unimaginable power of the Seelie Scepter and the Unseelie Throne like a dead, brittle branch, and in wrath, forced them away from the Ever-Dying shores.

I should mention he's really fond of humans. No one knows how he did it, but in the middle of a war that destroyed half the city, my uncle made sure only two ordinary mortals died. The Ever-Dying thought the hurricane and waterspout were natural disasters and mourned the loss of the London Bridge. The Mythos knew better, and the courts went really quiet for a while.

Five hundred years after that, an over-eager Fey prince decided to bolster his own reputation by taking my uncle down. He attacked in Dover, causing earthquakes and all kinds of mayhem, but my uncle did more than defeat him. Merlin dragged him back to his parents by his ear, and then burned the royal Seelie orchards to the ground. He ended thousands of years of unique and valuable horticulture in ash, and after that, no one attacked him anymore.

Merlin took one single apple seed home for his own use, by the way. That tree still grows on Bardsey Island, producing apples mysteriously immune to blight. You won't find another like it anywhere in the world.

I can only guess what kinds of stories Grey was told. Myrddin—who's never so much as lost his temper in my presence—became his own crazy legend. It tickled him silly, so when his cleric friend Geoffrey asked for permission to write up my uncle's favorite stories, of course my uncle said yes—on the condition that names were changed to protect the innocent.

Myrddin became Merlin, Caledfwlch became Caliburn (which eventually metamorphosed into Excalibur), and from there, Geoffrey made up a whole bunch of nonsense. Everyone who came after him added even more, and the legend grew into something spectacularly tentacular and fantastic. There was no round table, originally. Sorry to disappoint.

My uncle was pretty pleased by it. He adopted the name Merlin because it was funny, took to wearing ridiculous colors and pointed hats (which he said made him feel "wizardly"), and began collecting objects he thought might fit the Arthurian legends. If there weren't any, he invented them. So there's a round table *now*.

He's not scary. He's dangerous, but not to me. If the Hunt really was after this baby dragon, then there was no place I'd rather be than with my in-famous uncle, Merlin the Magician.

"He's not really your uncle," Grey accused. "You're too young."

"No, he's something like my great, great, great, great, great grandfather times a dozen, but we're so far removed by now that he prefers to be called uncle. And nobody in the family understood—or inherited—his sense of humor but me, for the record." I tripped on a loose stone and caught myself just in time to avoid squishing my passenger.

"I should leave you here. He doesn't like the Fey," said Grey.

Poor guy. "He'll like you just fine. You helped me. And unlike the Hunt, my uncle won't attack you unless you attack him first, and you're not going to do that, right? So just calm down."

As I neared the top, my view of the stars grew wavy, as if through heat rising from a sunbaked road. I stopped and swept my arm in front of me, and the distorted air parted like a curtain. Warm yellow light enveloped us. "Come on," I said, holding the way open.

He ducked through, so pale I almost felt sorry for him, and I followed after.

The clocks are always the first thing anybody notices. There are nearly fifteen hundred of them, one for each year Arthur has been asleep, and my uncle never bothers to set them all to the same time.

Out-of-sync ticktocks warred with distant chimes, echoing through an enormous dark tower that rose up and up above us into the gloom. The clocks shared space with recognizable reproductions of Pre-Raphaelite art and full-scale tapestries, all depicting Arthurian mythology. He had a few originals, too, including an enormous poster from Disney's *Sword in the Stone* and a couple of outfits from the 1967 film version of *Camelot*. It's all funny as hell to him.

Except for Guinevere, I might add. He hates the woman, even though she never existed, because she betrayed his precious Arthur. Not acceptable. Apparently. He's not too keen on Lancelot, either.

Grey gawped up. "Whoa."

"Follow me." I turned the clock nearest me to 4:50 (the year Arthur was born), and the section of stone beneath us rose smoothly into the air.

Grey didn't startle at that. He was too busy staring at the walls. "I thought this was supposed to be a tower of glass."

"Who would want to live in a tower of glass?" I said, smiling a little because my uncle had always added, *can't even do your business without people watching you wipe your ass!* My mother hadn't liked his language. Naturally, he'd immediately become my favorite person ever.

Grey clenched his jaw and swallowed so hard his ears bobbed. I fought a mad urge to pet him until he calmed down. It suddenly hit me that he felt . . . well, *young*. "Hey," I said. "How old are you?"

He scowled. "Why?"

I shrugged.

More scowls. "I'm seventy-eight. Why, dammit?"

Oh, he *was* young, for Fey, anyway. That essentially made him my age, developmentally. "I just thought you'd be older."

"What's that supposed to mean?" he demanded.

The stone kept moving, and faces both clock and painted watched us rise. "I just thought you were older. Acting all suave, with your own little portal and all. You know."

He crossed his arms. "No, I don't know."

I rolled my eyes. "You have a portal. A *portal*. That's like running into a twenty-three-year-old guy with his own Learjet. I was just curious, that's all."

Grey gave me the kind of look that normally precedes leaping out a window. "There's no reason," he said. "No reason at all. It doesn't matter. Let it go."

Woo-woo, Mister Mystery. "Fine, geez. Forget I said anything."

The stone stopped, flush with the floor of my uncle's lab, but our little trip had been for naught. My uncle wasn't here.

Thin glass tubing climbed the walls in shapes ordinary blown glass could never achieve, crawling with bubbles and fluids of all colors. Desks and tables filled the place haphazardly, piled with paperwork and bowls that boiled and stirred themselves. Several frogs with disproportionately huge eyes peered at us from bell jars, and Viking-esque gold gleamed in suspicious-looking piles.

"Ooh," said Grey, turning in a slow circle to take it all in.

"Uncle Merlin?" I don't know why I called. There was nowhere for him to hide up here, and there were no other rooms.

"What was he doing? Looting gravesites?" Grey leaned over a pile of mismatched earrings, wisely keeping his hands to himself.

"I have no idea. Everything he does relates to Arthur, somehow. Uncle Merlin?" No answer, of course.

"Well." Grey shrugged. "I suppose you could leave the dragon in one of those bell jars."

"No!"

"Why not? It didn't kill the frogs."

I took a huge, pre-yell breath before I realized he was teasing, and puffed it out with a glare. "Not funny."

He grinned at me and wandered over to a desk that featured an inexplicable pile of socks.

Whatever. I rolled my eyes and took a few aimless steps. "Uncle Merlin?"

A beam of light suddenly shot down from the ceiling overhead, and my uncle appeared. He was see-through, his edges fuzzy, all over blue. He smiled brightly to my right. "Hello, Katie."

There was no power. No warmth, no sense of a living thing. "Uncle?"

"I should tell you I can't respond to you, since I'm nothing but a recording." He adjusted his pointy hat. Today's selection was purple with big yellow stars. "I've left this here just in case something happens, which is silly, because something always happens, don't you agree?" He beamed over my right shoulder.

Grey walked up behind me. "You're kidding."

"Hush. It's a recording, and I don't know if it'll repeat," I said.

"But he looks so *goofy.*"

"Shh!"

"Katie, my dear, I'm certain that by now you've gotten my present." My uncle's projection folded his hands behind his back and leaned up on his toes. "I'm inordinately pleased with myself, as you can likely tell. After all, it isn't every day we manage to pull one over on the big bads, eh? Eh? Hahaha!"

Present? Suvi was a present?

"Big bads?" Grey said dryly.

"Shh."

My uncle was rocking the old-man look at the moment, and he tapped his bearded chin. "Of course, if you're *here*, then you probably didn't understand what I was doing, and you probably brought the Starling with you. Well. Blast it all, that wasn't what I wanted."

Tears stung my eyes. "Well, then you should have left a note, shouldn't you?" I knew he couldn't hear me. I knew, too, if he wasn't here, then he couldn't help me. Something had happened. As he said, something always does. It wasn't fair.

"If you *are* here, Katie, my dear, then I do have a suggestion." He smiled again. "Take him to the Crow King. I'll be there waiting for you."

"The who-king?" I said.

"Did I mention the Starling is sort of a prophesied . . . thing?" my uncle's image suddenly said, waving his hand vaguely. "They're pretty upset about it. And Katie, my dear, thank you." His smile faded. "There's no one else I could possibly trust with such a delicate creature, knowing you will not take advantage. I will see you at Bran's with the Starling in hand, sweet niece. Be careful. Be wise." The projection didn't disappear, but my uncle went still, smiling inanely and slightly to my right.

His faith failed to reassure me.

I looked in my bag. Vesuvius lay in a tiny circle, his long neck and tail curved against each other like a thin handle on a dragon purse. A scattering of shed scales glittered around him, and the outline of his wings was clearer than before. He huffed in his sleep, maybe reacting to the cool air outside his nest.

I zipped him up again. "What are we going to do?"

"We?" said Grey. "There is no 'we.'"

"Sure there is, and *we* are going to find my uncle."

Grey gave me a look. "You're crazy. You're both crazy, and now—"

"Hm," my uncle's projection suddenly said. "I almost forgot: The dragon might be grumpy, so do watch out."

And on cue, the grumpy dragon showed up.

Power washed over us, freezing us like bad things in bad dreams when you can't move your legs, and your arms grow too heavy, and the urge to *run* gives you tunnel vision even though you *cannot do anything.*

The adult dragon poured into our reality like a balloon filling with terror instead of air. Burnt-brick red, it filled the space in the lab, smashing equipment and furniture against the walls, flattening the poor frogs, and curling its insanely long tail around its body like a cat. Long and supple, its neck glimmered with ruby scales all the way up to its long, narrow head. It sported horns that glittered like diamond dust, and teeth that shone like knives. Its eyes were black, intent, and intelligent.

And it was dying.

Smoke rose in a black, sickly funnel from its mouth, and sticky blood that smelled like charcoal dripped between its teeth and from its torn sides to pool on the floor. Its claws shook as it reached for us, black talons gleaming and each one larger than a T. rex's tooth.

Power flashed from Grey, a brief blink of light.

"Do not fight me, child of the grasses," said the dragon in a deep and terrible engine of a voice, and his compulsion washed through us like unpleasant dishwater. "I have words for you this night. Find the Starling child." Grey choked something, but the dragon couldn't care less what he had to say. Compulsory magic stole our breath, wouldn't let us close our eyes. "Find him and keep him safe."

Every word slammed through me.

The dragon shuddered with such violence that the tower shook with him, and plaster dust rained down. "Find the Starling child," said the dragon again, curling his long neck down so his wheelbarrow-wide head lay on the stones in front of us. "Do this, and he will . . ." His voice trailed off, and he died.

So much *presence* left with him. The essence of a powerful, beautiful being, old and wise and experienced, evaporated, and when he left, there was a vacuum. The world was *less*. We were less, for having lost him.

"Damned stinking rotten-egg slime!" Grey shouted at the top of his lungs.

I wasn't so much with him on this one. I swayed in place, waved my hand, meaning nothing, everything. The bag hugged my side, its tiny occupant evidently still asleep. That was good. I didn't want him to see the dead dragon. For all I knew, this was his father. "Grey," I whispered.

Grey went to his knees, stood, and fell again. He punched the floor with his fist.

I knelt more carefully and touched the dragon's head. It was too warm, and I had to pull my hand back. Tears made me blink more. "He's dead."

"Foul worm-sucking ash-wig!" said Grey.

Grief can laugh. I know this. "Ash-wig? What the hell?"

"An ash-wig is an individual who goes through other people's garbage for blackmail and gets filth all over his hair," Grey said like a college professor. "I hate dragons. We have to do it, you know. That spell was binding. We have to go do whatever he's talking about."

"Um, Grey?" I patted my bag. "I think we already did. Starling child, boom."

"Wrong. What the dead dragon meant is bigger than that. We have to actually make sure the baby dragon is safe, permanently. If we try to do anything else, the spell will compel us back."

Hm. "Well. I think the next step hasn't changed. We need to find this Crow King. Find him, and we find my uncle." I was almost steady enough to walk on my own two feet.

"No, because that's insane," said Grey.

"Like this isn't insane?" I waved at the whole lab and did a double take to see big-eyed frogs wriggling out from under the dragon's corpse. Those were some hearty amphibians.

"I've heard of him. He's some kind of collector. *Col-lec-tor*," Grey slowed the word for my benefit. "He'll take your baby dragon if he sees him."

That did give me pause. "There's nowhere safe to put him, Grey. And my uncle can sort this out. Who else could? Besides, I've never heard of this Crow guy. He can't be a big deal. What's the worst thing that can happen?"

He threw his hands in the air. "You're mad. Completely, utterly, bat-shittingly mad."

"Bat-shittingly?" Well, that did it. Here we were, entangled in *literal* draconian conspiracies, and now Grey was making up words. I started to giggle.

"This isn't funny!" Grey stared up at me from the floor.

"It's laugh or cry, right?" I couldn't stop giggling. *Bat-shittingly* was going on my vocabulary list.

"Or rage and rant. I prefer ranting," said Grey.

"Well, I prefer laughing. So! Are we going, or not? Come on. It's like you've never been on an adventure before." I nudged him with my toe, which was a mistake, because my balance hadn't returned and I fell on my ass. "There and back again?"

"This isn't *The Hobbit*."

"Close enough. We need answers. Come on. We're going to see some guy who calls himself the Crow King, for real, in this day and age. It'll make a really neat story someday."

"If we survive," he intoned.

"I will have no wussing out on my watch. Up."

Grey groaned and rubbed his face. "Wussing. Really?"

I touched the dead dragon's head again.

He was still warm, uncomfortably so, but his scales were as smooth as polished glass, and fading power thrummed beneath them. Maybe I was spelled, or maybe I just had an appreciation for rare creatures, but this being had clearly been murdered. He was one more wonder gone from the world. At least he'd died here. Out there, who knows what would have scavenged his corpse?

Grey dusted off his knees. "This whole thing is insane. It's not the 900s anymore. People don't behave like this."

I scoffed. "The 900s. *Everybody* talks about the 900s like they were so great, but neither of us were there."

He huffed, then pulled the portal coin out of his pocket.

"Whoa." I touched his arm. "We've already jumped around the world twice. If this collector-king does something whack, I'd rather save whatever power you have left for an escape."

He shrugged. "I have enough to get us out again."

I peered at him. He'd essentially just told me his Learjet could fly into space. "You have that much power?"

He looked at the simple silver disk in his hand. "Yes." His face twisted. Some kind of war was happening inside his head, and I had no idea what it was. "Let the cards fall where they may," he said with quintessential Fey dramatics, and dropped the coin.

CHAPTER 3

THE CROW KING

Maybe I had made the wrong decision.

Bran's castle stood exactly where an old Ever-Dying castle once had, though from the placard, the human version had survived only twenty years before burning down. The world of the Mythos and the world of the Ever-Dying often build in the same places. We just shifted our buildings to exist a few seconds apart from the ones humans build, technically in the same place, but not at the same time. Of course, after a while, we figured out it wasn't actually the same place anymore, either.

We'd successfully created parallel worlds. We're big on parallels in magic. It saves so much trouble, and our worlds are in much better condition than yours.

"This is such a bad idea," Grey said.

Looking at this place, I had to agree. The Crow King went for "imposing," evidently. All black stone, it rose in unsubtle phallic splendor, lambent windows spreading red-gold light into the night sky, and its walls carved with deep, jagged runes bigger than a Volkswagen Bug.

The wards on this place were completely out of bounds. Understand, there are wards, and then there are *wards*. These were high-class, royalty-level,

Fort-Knox-crazy wards, so thick that even though the magic in my blood let me see this hidden castle, it appeared all fuzzy and out of focus.

Grey turned in a slow circle. While the night was beautiful, and tiny towns lit it up in the distance, none came close to this isolated tower. That was weird. Magic users usually cluster around bastions of power like moths around a flame.

"Where is everybody?" asked Grey.

Well, not here, apparently. "No idea. Why have I never heard of this guy?"

"Something about this whole situation is hinky," said Grey.

"Hinky?" I stared at him. "Hinky? Really?"

"That's the technical term," he deadpanned. "Are you sure we should do this?"

Lying would do no good. "No. But my uncle said to come here, and now there's a dead dragon we need to take care of—"

"*We* need to take care of it?"

"—not to mention making the baby safe, so we need the help. I don't know what else to do. Do you?"

"Pretty weak, Katie," said Grey.

Now wasn't the time to think about how much I liked the way he said my name.

I pulled my bag's strap over my head and across my body to secure it. "No sense waiting."

"I beg to differ," Grey said, but he followed me as I climbed the hill. "What's with this day and steep inclines, anyway?"

I ignored this. "It should be pretty simple. We knock on the door, ask if my uncle is there, and if he's not, we leave."

"I'm sure." Grey rubbed his arms as if cold. He was probably more sensitive to the go-away wards than I was. "It will absolutely be that simple, because it's just like borrowing a cup of sugar from a sweet old lady. Seriously, how long *have* you been out of the magical world?"

I didn't answer him. I didn't feel like it. So there.

I'd never encountered such an unwelcoming place. This Crow King had put up mockeries where the human castle's outer walls once stood: jutting boulders like leaning teeth, too large for gravestones, scattered like drunken thoughts. I shuddered when we passed them, these ancient earth's bones, these stones that screamed the unrelenting fluidity of time and the finiteness of mortal lives, the briefness of all lifespans and the hollow spots they left behind.

I already hated the place and hadn't even hit the front door. "Maybe this is a bad idea," I said weakly.

Grey grabbed my arm.

"Hey!" I protested.

"Look!" he said, pointing.

The way behind us had closed.

A wall of solid blackness hid our path, like curtains, but it didn't feel solid. My eyes played tricks on me, but I sensed movement—solid black against solid black, impossible to see, and definitely not products of my imagination.

We hadn't been closed off by a barrier. That was a whole dark world out there, some new and different dimension I didn't know. I told you we're big on parallel worlds. The Crow King had his own pocket-dimension all to him-self—himself and whatever dark things moved in that total night.

"The stars are gone," Grey said in a tiny voice, and he swayed on his feet.

"Grey," I said as evenly as I could. "Are you okay?"

"For now." He didn't look at me.

Fey don't do well completely separated from natural light, no, they do not, and whatever existed here that let us see was *not light*. Screw this. He needed to Learjet the hell away from here. "Use your portal. Leave."

"I can't." He inhaled through his teeth, sweat dripping down his face. "Whatever . . . whatever this is, it's overcome me. Darkness, Katie. It's of the Darkness. I can't."

Oh, crapburgers with brains for breakfast.

Seven Peoples of the Earth. Kin was one; the Fey were one; Darkness was another, and the Darkness and Fey lived as predator and prey. Darkness magic just sort of ate Fey magic up, devoured and destroyed those who bore it. Fey could grow addicted even as it drained them dry.

This just got better and better! "Grey. Look at me. We've got to keep moving."

"We should go back," he said like a small child, and it was my turn to grab his arm and pull. There was no going back, not that way. I'm Kin, and I may not be very powerful, but I wouldn't be alive at all if I didn't have a keen sense of danger. Whatever was out there would eat us. We dared not go back that way.

"Come on. You can do it." I dragged him, clawing my way up the absurdly steep hill with my free hand, my dragon-baby bag secured with the strap diagonally across my chest. The air seemed thin here, or maybe the composition was slightly different. Winded, muscles shaking, I wiped sweat from my eyes and wondered if the Crow King's front doors actually did undulate like some whacked-out hologram or if I was just fading faster than I thought.

Grey leaned against me, shuddering, with a look of intense concentration, so he didn't see the eyes. Tiny red points gleamed all over the tower, paired like crows' eyes, except the small black shapes behind them couldn't be crows. As far as I'm aware, eye glow is not standard crow behavior.

Whatever they were, they weren't attacking, so I took the opportunity and knocked.

It sounded so small, like knocking on stone, though my knuckles didn't sting. I raised my hand to knock again, and then the door opened.

I saw a thing. Dark red, skin cracked like the desert, huge blue eyes and small black horns, shockingly and horrifyingly beautiful in some deep and wild way that dizzied me, as if I'd tried to see in four dimensions.

I closed my eyes tightly and shook my head. Nope. No member of the Darkness was going to overwhelm me that easily. I was Katherine Aelwen Lin, descendent of Myrddin the Wizard, and I would not be had.

I opened my eyes again and found something completely different.

He was the handsomest man I'd ever seen, in a Hollywood-piratey-rogue kind of way. Thick, rumpled black hair, deep blue eyes and a jawline I could crack walnuts on. Broad shoulders and chest well defined in his too-tight tee, he stood there in casual but expensive jeans, with bare feet, one thumb in his pocket, and looked at us with a combination of amusement and wariness.

Either this was fake and the red guy was real, or the red guy was fake and this guy was real. Either way, we were in over our heads. "Hi," I said, like one does.

The man looked us both up and down with equal scrutiny and arched one perfect eyebrow. "I give up. What *are* a high-bred Kin woman and an Unseelie prince doing on my doorstep?"

Prince?

You know, I could poke at that later. This guy's burr was amazing, charming, sensual, and delightful, and the way he spoke put me in mind of the rhythm of ravens and writing desks. I hated this place even more. "We need help."

He made an amused sound. "You do indeed, though how you came to need it in this place is a mystery beyond even me."

I knew how: the baby dragon in my bag, busting through magical walls and wards since 4 o'clock this afternoon. I swallowed hard and did not offer that information.

The Crow King stepped aside and held the creaking door wide. "However you came to be here, you'd best come inside now. I'd hate to think what the bone collectors would do with you if they caught you tonight."

Bone collectors. Those sounded fun.

Grey hung against me, head down, face hidden by his hair, and in spite of warnings of bone collectors (whatever *those* were), I didn't want to take him in. This felt like handing a silvery butterfly over to a big, black spider.

His knees buckled. He caught himself, but barely.

The starless sky was doing more damage than anything else. We had to find an exit. I braced myself and walked him inside.

The door shut behind us and echoed through the stone of the hall and the tower above. I guess my knock had been more obvious than I thought. The entrance hall was dark, windowless, lit by three solitary torches, but not by fire: they were sticks with glowing blue stones roped to them, utterly devoid of heat.

"May I offer you something?" said the Crow King, walking past me with heavy grace that didn't fit the jeans-and-tee-shirt look at all, but went with bare feet just fine. I knew, somehow, this guy could move *fast* when he wanted. Noted.

"No, thank you. I'm sorry, but we didn't mean to drop in like this."

"So I gathered. You're not dressed for it." Over his toned shoulder, he cast a smile at me that was all teeth, too many teeth, but when I blinked, they looked perfectly ordinary again. Just a little too late for comfort, but hey, he was trying.

Grey's feet dragged, but he put less of his weight on me. Maybe he was recovering. "We're looking for someone," I pressed.

I couldn't tell what was on the thin carpet, thrown onto the floor's cold stone. Whatever the symbols were, they wriggled, and the Crow King was already halfway across it. "Unless you were looking for me, I'd say you're lost." He sounded far more amused than wary now.

I wanted to be cleverer about this, but I just didn't have the strength. "We're looking for the Kin wizard Myrddin. He said he'd be here."

The Crow King stopped, his toes just over the edge of the wriggling carpet, and turned his face to the right as if to hear me more clearly. "He told you he was here? How and when did he do that?"

He spoke like a king.

Authority is something few people possess. This breed was inherent, in-born, and carried with it an unspoken promise of retribution if faced with defiance. I doubted this Crow King did it intentionally. I was being treated to a bare hint, a glimpse of the strong arm beneath his casual exterior.

"He left me a message," I said vaguely.

"Did he? Is this message still discoverable?"

Oh, totally, and I forwarded it to the police, and by the way, the army's coming. "Yes. Absolutely."

Shadow hid his eyes, but his profile's smile grew satisfied. "Absolutely, as you say. Follow me." He resumed his slow, controlled walk.

"We are so screwed," Grey whispered in my ear, just a little too loudly.

"Shh," I told him.

Up ahead, swallowed by the dark, the Crow King chuckled.

The low-ceilinged hall continued on, marked by doors bolted closed with wide, thin metal bars. Odd scents wafted from some: burning scents, flowering scents, scents like smelted copper or fresh, warm laundry.

There were sounds, too, distant and muffled. Were they voices? Machinery in need of oil? Tormented souls? A chorus of roasting gnomes?

"I offer you my hospitality," said the Crow King, padding ahead of us silently. "I have tea for the coward and wine for the brave." He stopped at a door with golden hinges in the shape of dragons' claws. "Enter with my blessing."

I had no idea where we were now relative to the hill. It seemed we'd gone too far to be walking on the same straight plane anymore. "Thank you. I'll take the coward's route."

He laughed and opened the door, and his amused gaze had weight, like full-body fetters. I resisted the urge to hold Grey between us like a privacy curtain.

Grey balked the second we walked through the door. "Birds?" he said.

Birds, indeed. The crows, I might have expected. Stuffed ones sat next to live ones that perched on black statue-crows with gleaming red eyes.

But there were also stuffed vultures casting misshapen shadows. Eagles frozen in flight with beaks open and wings wide. A roc's whole head took up an entire corner farthest from the fireplace, freakish with lidless eyes. Shelves, side tables, and spare seating all displayed birds, alive and dead, watching our entrance in eerie silence, and only some great magical power prevented the whole place from being covered in droppings and stench.

There was no stench. There also wasn't the homey, woody smell of a fire. The fireplace held a pile of glowing red stones, giving not quite as much light as a small fire would.

The faint and pleasant smell of grilled meat did not really comfort me. I led Grey over to the two love seats facing each other in front of the fireplace. A half-eaten meal of steak and some kind of yam sat abandoned on a small table from when its devourer came to admit us. We sat across from it.

The Crow King settled back in place and resumed his meal with slow consideration, as if even the very act of cutting steak held some vast and powerful pleasure. He took a bite with his eyes on mine, a whole level beyond flirting. "You're blushing," he said.

I cleared my throat. "I just climbed a hill dragging this guy. That'd be why."

"You don't sound . . . local." A teasing smile shaped his lips as he took another bite.

He was fishing for something. "Please forgive me, Crow King, I don't mean to be rude, but we really need to know if Myrddin's here or not."

"Oh, he's here." Another bite of steak, followed by a chaser of red wine in a goblet that probably cost more than my car. His Adam's apple moved with each swallow, and even that was distracting, so I looked down at the plate.

I waited. He added nothing.

"So . . . can we see him?" I said.

"No. Not without an even trade." He dabbed his mouth with a red cloth.

Oh, come *on*. "What trade?" He was going to ask for Grey. I knew it. Or some of his hair, or some wonky hoodoo garbage.

"You're his great, great, great—oh, I'd say in the neighborhood of fiftieth generation granddaughter, yes?"

I opened my mouth and shut it with a snap. "Um," I said, intelligently.

"I rarely have a chance to sample blood such as yours and his in a twenty-four-hour period," said the Crow King, who, by the way, never freaking blinked. "I intend not to let this opportunity pass without making use of it."

"Um," I quipped, ever brilliant.

"Don't worry." He smiled, a narrow-eyed, tight-lipped thing that managed to worm its way under my skin like good sex and bad wine. "I won't hurt you! I'm not that kind of collector. You'll leave much the same as you are now. Fears allayed?"

"No. Noooo, they are not." I waved my finger, not exactly pointing it at him. "They are very much not allayed!"

"Understandable." The Crow King finished his wine. "Perhaps you are squeamish about blood. Ah, but I have an alternative."

"Oh," I said. "That's good. Your Highness—"

"Please call me Bran."

"Bran?"

I might have squawked it, because he laughed. "The father of your child should at least be on a first-name basis with you."

No, this was not happening. Was not. Denied.

I put my face in my hands, seriously debating whether the spooky dark things eating me would be worse than this, and vowing off all magic-users for the rest of my life (again) once this was over. I knew this guy was old guard, but seriously? He wanted to "get" a child by me? Really? This was a lateral move from *give me your firstborn or I'll turn your family into geese!* What was I supposed to do here?

My bag squeaked.

"What is that?" said Bran, putting down his silverware with a bang.

I tried so hard for a poker face. "A bag."

"I can see that. What's inside it?" Bran leaned back now, turning slightly to keep his knees further away from me.

Well, wasn't that interesting? "Wouldn't you like to know?" I said, reverting to the bonny wee age of seven.

Suvi squeaked again, more demandingly. He must have used all the strength in his tiny body to push against the nylon, distending it like a pregnant belly, and I began to fear he'd hurt himself.

"Better let him out," said Grey, whose skin was beginning to match his name. His eyes, however, glinted, grinned, communicated something in every way but a wink, as if we had some great secret plan.

I looked at my bag.

Vesuvius burrowed around in there, growling and huffing. He was going to worm his way out eventually.

Bran said nothing, his eyes huge. Subtly, he scooted toward the far end of his couch.

Not subtle enough. I opened the bag.

Vesuvius flew out like an insane firecracker, displaying brand-new wings and spraying sparks.

Bran threw himself backward with an inhuman roar, and Grey stood with his teeth bared, his hair flying up and back in a display of stunning magic. With one graceful catch-and-throw motion, he summoned all those sparks into his hand and tossed them in Bran's face.

The Crow King howled and burst into flame all over, *all over,* and flipped wildly against the walls like a cat frantically trying to climb out of a bathtub. The live birds all took to the air, filling it with feathers and claws and squawking, and *then*, because it just wasn't creepy enough, the stuffed birds all began to scream.

I said some really foul words and scrambled backward over the love seat, crouching in a heap behind it with my hands over my head. Something popped, and feathers and sawdust exploded over the top of the loveseat to fall like snow all around me.

I had to see and peeked around the loveseat's base just in time to see more stuffed birds popping. They screamed, distended, and exploded, dried parts flying everywhere, glass eyeballs rolling on the floor.

Grey drew himself to his full height.

Even his lips had lost color, but his eyes gleamed like polished silver. Hands shaking, power dancing beneath his skin like embers, he sang a word.

A word that rang like the toll of a bell. A word that shook the whole room with one ringing gong, a word that rose in my soul like a motif, an anthem I *had* to sing with and a tune I *had* to dance to and a song I *had* to dream by, a word I could feast on as my only sustenance if only I could hear it forever.

Music was his magic. Music. What did that mean? That made him a particular kind of Fey, and I couldn't think—

The eagles exploded, all right in a row, and I ducked and covered my head —but I didn't have to. Grey's note had raised an invisible wall.

Briefly spared the rain of sawdust, I looked around. Bran was gone. Maybe he'd burned to ash. Maybe the moon is cheese, too, you never know.

I grabbed Grey's arm. "Time to go, Pavarotti!"

He shook his head, doubled over and barely breathing, but I would not be stopped. I dragged him, slipping on the flood of lint, sawdust, and feathers, hit the door, and found it locked.

It wouldn't budge. Would not open. Would not.

I kicked it. "Damn you, Bran, let us out!"

No sign of my would-be fecundator appeared, and Grey knelt against the door, visibly spent. The lights that had danced beneath his skin were gone. He was done.

"Open the damn door!" I screamed, and the roc's head chose just that moment to blow.

A tidal wave of sawdust and wet, meaty, horribly red stuff smacked into Grey's invisible wall and rose right over the top to deluge us with all the sloppy enthusiasm of a puppy left alone all day. Feathers. Wet things. An eyeball the size of a soccer ball and definitely not glass splatted right on my foot, and I kicked it away with a scream.

Oh, that was not a scream of fear, but of raw, temperature-altering rage. If a certain Crow King had made his appearance right then, I would have done everything in my limited power to put his eyes on the ground along with the roc's.

"Katie?"

I spun.

My uncle stood in the ragged remains of the roc's neck stump as if he'd risen out of the floor. His purple robe covered in big, goofy stars and unspeakable gore, tiny strips of flesh quivering on every surface, he offered me an enormously wizard-esque smile and held out his arms as if in welcome. "Hello!"

I coughed and waved a cloud of sawdust out of my face. "Uncle?"

He plucked a tiny strip of meat from his shoulder and eyed it before tossing it to the floor. "My dear, you are a miracle worker. Starling? Come here, baby, it's all right."

He spoke with perfect paternal prerogative, and Suvi obediently flew out of the rafters. He landed in my uncle's outstretched hand with surprising grace, then clawed up his arm with none. Merlin made interesting faces as Suvi's needle-sharp claws achieved traction.

"What . . . you . . . you were in the roc?" I gawked at him.

"Why, yes. Bran rather thought I'd grow amicable if he had me in there for a while." Merlin tsk'd and ran his fingertips along Vesuvius's outstretched neck.

"But he put you in a bird's *head*," I said, struggling with this.

"Son of a bitch," Grey muttered at nothing in particular.

"Be polite," I said, in case he was aiming that at my uncle.

"It's all right, my dear, he's clearly had quite a day." Uncle Merlin stepped over the stuffed roc's neck, delicately picking bits of flesh off his robe. Suvi perched on his shoulder, gnawing to no effect a pink strip that hung off my uncle's ear. "Where is the old fellow?"

"Old f . . . Bran? Uh. We kind of set him on fire. And his birds. The stuffed ones. All of them, I think."

"That does follow," Merlin said thoughtfully. "They were centuries old, and all held together by his power. I suppose the break in his concentration was just too much. Poor fellow. I'll have to make that up to him somehow."

"Make it up to *him*?"

"Oh, my dear." Merlin gave me a fond, warm look. "Do understand. Bran is my friend."

"Friend?" I waved at the room filled with a crazy man's bird parts, and then pointed at myself. "He tried to get me pregnant!"

"He does that, yes." Merlin plucked more meat from his beard.

I threw my arms in the air. "And he kidnapped you! And put you in a bird!"

"Of course he did. He's a collector."

I leveled my finger at him. "Friends do not kidnap and impregnate each other!"

"They do when they're of the Darkness, my dear. It wasn't personal. It's simply how they relate. I assure you, were he actually our enemy, there would be no offer of hospitality, and no discussion involved. And if our lives are ever in danger, he would come to my aid and yours, as you are my family. Now, let me see—"

"I don't *want* him to come to my aid!" I yelled, waving my arms again.

"Did we kill him?" Grey looked up, his voice as rough as someone who hadn't sung for a long time and had just spent an hour belting out show tunes.

"No." Merlin looked at him with none of the fondness he showed me, the guarded look of one magical being to another. "He is ashamed at his natural appearance, but neither his magic nor his illusions can bear fire. Revealed, in startled pain, he fled. I doubt he's even injured."

"Oh, goody," I said. "He's fine, we're fine, we're all covered in meat. I want to go home, Uncle Merlin. I want to go *right now*."

Merlin's smile for me was the dawn after a cold nighttide. "Of course. I promise to make all of this up to you, as well. Let's go home." He snapped his fingers.

And we were gone.

CHAPTER 4

MERLIN'S DRAGON

My uncle makes really good cider.

Grey and I sat at his rustic wooden table, wrapped in hugely fluffy robes and wearing fuzzy slippers, and we sipped that steaming hot cider. It helped. I felt like it cleared the sawdust out of my brain as thoroughly as the bath had taken it out of my hair.

Grey looked significantly better, and I tried not to think too hard about how Uncle Merlin had revived him. Music-magic users tend to require very personal kinds of energy.

Merlin sat across from us, finally clean, while Suvi—the Starling— perched on his shoulder. "I suppose you'd like some answers."

We just looked at him. It was that kind of day.

Merlin sipped. "A very long time ago, the queen of dragonkind came to me, and she made me a lovely little offer. She had the gift of far-sight, you see, and she knew—or she guessed, which is effectively the same—that her family would one day be divided."

"The war between the reds and the blacks?" I said.

"They've been in their war of inheritance for generations now. It's all very messy, but that's beside the point. She knew—or guessed—that one day, someone would be hatched from her line who was neither red nor black in color."

Suvi ("Starling" was going to take me a while) was certainly neither of those. "Okay."

Merlin smiled. "She asked me if I would be willing to keep this little fellow safe if and when he was born. He *or* she, of course," he added in a murmur because I'd made a fuss about gendered pronouns when I was fourteen. "In return, she gave me the last of her far-sight—or very good guessing, whichever it may be—and died. This little fellow, being neither color, is set up to potentially heal the gap between the western dragon clans and rule both. Of course, there are quite a few dragons who have no interest in a change in the status quo."

"So the red dragon in your lab?"

"Was my friend, and a spy," said Merlin as he studied his drink, sad memory crinkling the skin around his eyes. "He is the reason I knew of the Starling's birth, and the one who stood in the breach after I had smuggled the baby out."

That was horrible. This whole thing was horrible. I watched Suvi, who huffed in kitten-like distress as he tried to find the most comfortable place on my uncle's shoulder. "What's going to happen to him?"

"He will remain with me until he's able to defend himself," said Merlin so casually that I knew he was up to something.

"What about the Wild Hunt?" said Grey.

"Now that I have separated you from the Starling's scent and power, they will not come after you, and they dare not come here at all. No, I think the old truces will hold. For now."

I shuddered. Unstable, this all felt unstable, like a tower getting ready to fall. "Just what are you planning, Uncle Merlin?"

"Well, I can hardly expect him to unite the western dragon clans without some extra tricks in his claws," Merlin said.

"What are you going to do, teach him magic?"

"Yes, but I won't be doing it alone. John, this is your chance."

For several weird seconds, I had no idea who he was talking to. Then I looked at Grey. "Your name is John?"

"It's Grey," he said firmly.

"John Barron McCarrig, heir to the Unseelie throne, currently in self-imposed exile and making his living as some kind of folksinger, or so the scuttlebutt goes," said Merlin, sharing people's secrets with the world. Well. With me.

"Does the scuttlebutt involve hitting on strange girls in confluxes?" I said.

Grey said nothing. He studied his mug.

"You have a chance to respond," my uncle said quietly. "Be more than you were born to be—part of this, something greater. Stand on your own feet. Do this, and your heritage will matter less."

"And I'm sure the chance of a connection between the Unseelie Throne and your tiny new king has nothing to do with the offer," Grey said bitterly.

Dragons and Fey were historically not friends. I couldn't imagine what it would mean for one of the Fey courts to do this. "Isn't that a little . . . I dunno." I squirmed. "Wouldn't people see this as an act of war?"

Merlin looked at me, and I made the mistake of fully meeting his eyes.

My uncle's eyes are blue. Just blue. But there's too much there, something like the depths of space there, like the incomprehensible wideness of the universe there, like a wonderful so-huge-it-gives-you-claustrophobia stretch of time and knowledge and faith there, and I made a tiny sound and looked away.

He touched my hand. "We must unify before it is too late, Katie. We must, and soon. There is so little time left."

He always said that. My parents said he did, and my grandparents, and everyone I knew just rolled their eyes.

But now. Suddenly, now. The gift of far-sight from a long-dead dragon queen, and now . . .

"I'll think about it," said Grey.

Merlin wisely did not push. "Spend the night, both of you. Be rested and refreshed. I will send you both home tomorrow. The Hunt will not have any interest in either of you while the Starling remains here." His immense gaze rested on Grey. "I will see you again in . . . oh, a few months, I think. Do enjoy Manhattan."

"Enjoy Manhattan, he says," Grey muttered. "I'm going to Chicago, so there."

"Of course you are," said Merlin gently.

I almost voiced it: if Grey came here in a few months like Merlin said, I might see him again.

I wanted to. Call me crazy, but I wanted to. I liked how he talked. I liked his stupid humor. I even liked his smile and his hair and his pouting looks and his long, clever fingers. I wanted to see him again. But I wouldn't say that. Couldn't appear eager. I sipped cider instead.

When Merlin led us to our rooms, Grey said nothing, but before he went in for the night, he looked back at me. He started to speak, then changed his mind—and as he retreated, his pale cheeks betrayed the tiniest hint of a blush.

Oh yeah. I *win*. All the points to Katie, lords and ladies.

Merlin walked beside me, thoughtful. My room was the same one I'd always had here, filled with my favorite posters, with wonderful old books, and with a dozen different laptops he'd scavenged for me just because he knew I liked them. "Trouble is coming, my dear Katie."

"I know, Uncle."

"You won't see it." He hugged me. "I guarantee that. Sleep well, my dear. Tomorrow, I'll give you a far better Christmas present before sending you home. I'm sorry I had to involve you."

"I'm glad you did." I hugged him back.

I lay in my bed for a very long time, staring up at the canopy. It was Fey-cloth, sheer, with tiny dancing sparks in it like distant fireflies. I wouldn't see this trouble he spoke about? So . . . I guess that meant it would happen after I was dead.

I wanted to feel good about that. I wanted to feel relieved, but I didn't.

Tomorrow would be a new day, a day that brought me back to New Hampshire, a day that forced me to face the fact that I missed this magical madness a little. Office work really paled in comparison to it all, no matter how normal. No matter how safe.

We must unify before it is too late. Maybe . . . maybe my uncle would want a hand raising the baby dragon. Maybe I should come back and just stay with him, hide out here from my embattled family instead of the States. Or maybe I should stop hiding at all. Maybe reconciling the life I wanted and the life I had was a good idea. Or maybe I was lonelier than I thought, and all these thoughts were absurd.

I wondered if Grey would get to see *too late* come to pass. Either way, I wouldn't. I didn't know how to feel.

My dreams were filled with dragon fire, and a bright white star outshone the flame.

NOTTE'S BOOK OF KNOWLEDGE

In the time before time, the First War ended the peace of the Peoples of the Earth. Driven and desperate, survivors bred for power and magic, and they succeeded—with a legacy too great for their mortal forms, and a homeworld they left in pieces.

Afraid, they turned to Naktam, the Lord of Night Whispers, oldest of them all, and begged for advice—for he was strangest, and the most resilient. He knew Death by name, and embodied the hunger of all worlds; thus it was he taught them to define by families, to use soul's desire and blood's prime powerto join those like themselves.

The Seven Peoples of the Earth—the Sun, the Darkness, the Guardians, the Fey, the Dream, the Kin, and the Ever-Dying who have no magic—came to find their own through blood and spirit, and choose the symbols to rally by. In time, simpler symbols were added for the sake of time and varying skill.

Today, the Seven Peoples remain strong, balanced, and free, and few there are who fight this many-reined yoke.

THE SUN

Hunger: Hhealing.

Prime power: Light and heat.

Homeworld: Zenith, which is very hot, has numerous major stars, and is clean, regimented, and always welcomes those who are sick and require succor.

The People of the Sun bred for fire, light, qne heat, as a means to burn away infection and evil. This power grows over time; toward the end of their natural lifespan, their physical forms can no longer take the strain of magic coursing through them, and those who are the most ancient and venerated grow hotter, and hotter, and eventually explode into ash.

THE DARKNESS

Hunger: Hunger itself.

Prime power: Darkness.

Homeworld: Umbra, in which is no light at all—it *cannot* be perceived or felt in that place, except in small pockets which its Lord may design.

Those who are of the Darkness *hunger*. Most eat; some collect. There are those who can and do devour anything, including plague, radiation, and the dead. The Fey, in particular, are much prized, their magic unique for whatever the Throne and Scepter do to it before sending it back out.

Toward the end of their natural lifespan, their own forms can no longer satisfy their aching, empty need. Those who are the most ancient and venerated grow more shadowed, less substantial, and eventually fade like mist in morning sun..

THE GUARDIANS

Hunger: Protection.

Prime power: Resistance.

World: Officially, none.

Guardians are driven to protect. This need can attach itself to anything; there are sphinxes still guarding tombs deep underground, where they will remain until they die.

Something terrible happened in the First War, and those Guardians who remain are uniformly mad. Most still function amoung the Peoples, but rumors say the most powerful are locked away for the safety of all.

The Guardians are wildly varied in terms of natural lifespan. Some fairies live months; dragsons can live for centuries. The Saqalu, who inspired the four-winged symbol of the People of the Guardians, did not age.

However, no one lives forever; the Saqalu are gone, now called the Hashritu, the Broken, and are lost to all but memory.

THE FEY

Hunger: Curiosity.

Prime power: Creation.

World: The Silver Dawning, divided between the Seelie Scepter and Unseelie Throne.

The Fey, flighty and mercurial, often discover and build only to abandon. They are in part driven by an unnatural need to reclaim the magic stolen from them; all their power, from birth, is channeled until the Throne and Scepter, there to be distributed and wielded as needed to keep their People alive. Mostly, though, the Fey are driven by curiosity. *Can I make it work?* is eye-rollingly funny as a trope.

Alone among the Seven Peoples, the Fey must seek magic outside of themselves, or starve; it is a skill learned to weave it from others, from emotion or intimacy, from applause or anguish. Toward the end of their natural lifespan, they lose the ability to process these stolen strands of power. Their bodies grow cool, and still; they become smooth, pale stone, without blemish, and without life. When Fey reach the natural end of their lives, they leave behind them soulless statues of themselves, echoes of the beauty they once held.

THE DREAM

Hunger: Dreams.

Prime power: The influence and digestion of the unconscious mind.

World: The Plane of Dreams, guarded by ambulant trees, home to complete silence.

The Dream are rarely seen. They withrew from the horrors of the First War, and now dwell between realms, living in the walls that divide wake and sleep. Some taste nightmares and build them to madness; some share sweetness and encourage hope.

Their lifespans are unknown. The end of their natural existence is unknown. Inheritors of uneasy flesh, they have lost the ability to manifest sharply in our world for more than moments of time, and it remains unclear if they can ever rejoin those who truly live.

THE KIN

Hunger: Varied.

Prime power: Varied.

World: All worlds, but primarily the human Earth.

The majority of Kin appear human, and are the source of all tales of humans who wield such power. They aren't one thing or another, neither fish nor flesh nor good red herring, but the legacy of many Peoples, who nevertheless rarely recognize Kin as their own. Due to unpredictable genetics, Kin powers vary wildly.

The Kin were once trafficked. They themselves could be used to increase the numbers of an identifiable People progeny, and so Kin were taken, used, and discardded—until nine brave families stepped forward to claim the Kin's place upon the Great Wheel. Lin, Blackwood, Lester, Sims, Doe, Yang, Bard, Roth, and Williams: may their names never be forgotten! Those who had no home now do, a People and a power and presence to be respected.

THE EVER-DYING

Hunger: Discovery.

Prime power: None.

World: Earth.

From the viewpoint of the magical among the Mythos, humans are dying from the moment they're born. They are horrifyingly short-lived. Anything can kill them; worse tet, they have no magic, and can neither wield nor perceive its use.

They can, however, reproduce at a rate rarely seen outside of rabbits.

Notte, Naktam who chose the Peoples, the Lord of the Night Whispers, regards the Ever-Dying as precious, for only they can become his children. His intervention and protection enabled their growth, and ensured their place on the Wheel even though they have no magic.

THE LOST

Hunger: Unknown.

Prime power: Terrible.

World: Unknown.

"Lost" is a misnomer. Tthe Scepter and the Fey saw that many did not fit into the sillos of the Seven Peoples of the Earth, and so tried to claim them. After all, their magic could continue to power the Silver Dawning.

This turned out to be a bad idea. Some beings could be claimed, yes, and their magic stolen, but the rest...

Gods. Demons. Psychopomps. Those things which eschew names and descriptions as worthless and ill-fitted. Many live outside of reality in the Void; too, are those who are not native to Earth, even as it was before it shattered. Of these, less said is better said. They are frightening, for none know what drives them.

AMONG THE MYTHOS, WHO ARE YOU?

No one is defined by their People, any more than an ethnicity or culture determines who a person is, but it does influence environment and options. Understanding this ancient rubric is the first step into this world, and explains why these beings always introduce themselves thus: **Among the Mythos, I am [People,] called [name.] Who are you?**

LEXICON OF THE MYTHOS
IN WHICH IS LISTED NAMES AND TERMS

CHARACTERS

Bran: Prince of the People of the Darkness. Of the Shadow's Breath, he is powerful and beautiful—though for *some* reason, he prefers appearing in his human guise instead of as his enormous, seven-foot-tall, horned, brick-red self.

Darrin: A human number-cruncher at Katie's workplace. Don't worry, he wasn't that into her, either.

Grey: *Grey* is the term for Fey who have been cut off from The Scepter and The Throne as an ultimate form of punishment. Most Fey thus banished starve from loss of magic and die. John Barron Grey, *né* John Barron McCarrig, runaway Unseelie prince and heir to The Throne, said *screw that*, and made the name a point of honor.

Katie: Born Katherine Aelwen Lin. Merlin's niece (many times removed), she currently lives in New England, having fled her home in Wales. She's actually a lot more powerful than she thinks she is, but she can't afford to acknowledge it; there's too heavy an emphasis on "important" Kin bloodlines and offspring. Katie wants no part of the drama of the magical world, and has no plans to go back.

Kyle: Just a shout-out to some beloved neighbors and life-long friends of the author.

Merlin: A unique member of the Kin. He's thousands of years old and incredibly powerful. He's also the progenitor of the Lin family, which is one of the nine "important" families among the Kin. Afflicted with Very Good Guessing, Merlin has learned the art of moving through the world with a sanity-preserving sense of humor.

Sharada (Queen of Dragon Kind): The last dragon regent before the western dragon clans split over the color of their scales. She had the gift of far-sight, or Very Good Guessing, and was able to pass that on to Merlin before she died. She prophesied that one day, a baby dragon with diamond-hued form would appear to reunite her feuding offspring. She called that prophesied baby the Starling Child.

Suvi: He's *just a baby*. Also known as Vesuvius, also known as the Starling Child, Suvi is the baby dragon prophesied by Sharada to reunite the warring Black and Red dragons. As no one knows precisely how he's going to do this, the attempts to both kidnap and kill him have been extreme. He lives with Merlin, learning just what it means to carry responsibility in the world. Also, he thinks Katie Lin is his mom.

TERMS

Bone-Collectors: Bone collectors are a species of wild animal that populates the worlds of The Darkness, primarily Umbra. No one outside of Umbra knows much about them since they exist in complete darkness; what we do know is they're predators, very fast, and only interested in extracting and eating bone. They're considered scavengers among members of The Darkness, who are generally able to ignore them through power or a general lack of bones.

Conflux: A conflux is a travel station where one may legally cross country and world borders via the magical version of quantum entanglement. Their use requires a ticket; local government runs them, collecting the funds for public works. Confluxes can be entered by anyone, and are built with a natural pull for anyone with magic—so to avoid accidental human discovery, conflux entry-points are designed to be absolutely repulsive, and not good at all for shelter.

Bardsey Island: An actual island in Wales (look it up!) and the home of Myrddin, according to legend. It does, indeed, have a unique kind of apple tree, immune to blight.

Dragon: Dragons are some of the most dangerous beings among the Mythos. They are also unusual in that they can fall into *two* Peoples depending on choice. All dragons have an insatiable hunger and desire to collect things (the Darkness); all dragons also have the power to heal, and manipulate light (the Sun). Which People claims them is entirely individually decided.

Future-Sight: See Very Good Guessing.

Gorgades: Friendly and blue-furred, gorgades have a culture focused on business acumen, and combined with remarkable healing powers, tend to be quietly and efficiently rich. Insular, they don't bother with arts or entertainment from outside their own ranks, and only purchase homes on their islands, which are located off the Atlantic coast of Africa. Their healing powers place them in the People of the Sun.

Fey Portal: Transportation magic, completely different from Confluxes. A

Fey Portal essentially creates shortcuts by going through dimensional walls, carrying its bearer *through* the Void. This requires a huge amount of power, directly provided by the Throne or Scepter, and even most among the Fey can't control them well. They usually come in the form of a smalls portable item, like a coin.

Roc: An absolutely enormous bird, rare not due to predation, but due to the fact that Earth-based ecology can only support one within a reasonably large distance. Parts of a roc's bod are considered collector's items because they are incredibly difficult to kill—and by the fact that they tend to eat the remains of their own, leaving nothing to collect.

Shadow's Breath: Among the People of The Darkness, and currently the Darkness' rulers. They've been called many names: shadow-djinn, demons, nightmares, evil spirits, but most of this is honestly just humans trying to make sense of something scary, beautiful, and dangerous. Generally enormous, dark-brick-red in color, and covered in cracks with light flickering deep inside.

Very Good Guessing: A form of prophecy. The way future-sight works in the world of the Mythos is complicated. Those who can *see* say that the future looks like glowing strands tangled together, constantly moving and changing; every choice seems to alter what comes next. They call it the Tapestry.

The Void: The strange space through which Fey portals travel. What is it? Empty. What's there? Gods. It is... not a safe place. It's long been thought that puncturing holes in it to travel through is a less than wise activity, but nothing's gone wrong yet.

Wild Hunt: A contingent of young and rebellious demigods. They are not worshipped, and neither are their parents; they dislike the Void, where true gods live, and somehow what began as "go out and have fun" eventually became "kill what you find, especially if it's a challenge." They're deeply feared, and because of their power, can access all worlds—though fortunately, they usually avoid Earth. Humans make really lousy prey.

Want more? There is a full wiki on https://ruthannereid.com/. Enjoy!

NO ONE WRITES ALONE

I wrote this in a time when I feared I could Never Write Anything Good Again (a phase all writers enter, often more than once), yet thanks to the encouragement of others, I somehow made it through. Simply put, this little novelette wouldn't exist without Cameron, Nikki, and Kelli.

Celine and Bennett: You two have to be the most faithful beta readers in the world. I can't believe you're not sick of me yet.

Taylor and Gabby fell in love with Bran, which is good, because I wasn't sure yet if I liked him.

And as always, my husband provided the best backup, sounding board, and late-night encouragement a woman could want. Love you, Duane.

ABOUT THE AUTHOR

A bestselling author, Ruthanne Reid has led panels on world-building, taught courses on plot and character development, and been the keynote speaker for the Write Practice Retreat. Author of nine books and dozens of short stories, she makes daily videos to help other creatives get unblocked and into a healthy habit of creation.

Ruthanne has lived in her head since childhood, when she used up her mom's red typewriter ribbon writing a story about a pony princess and a genocidal snake-kingdom. When she isn't reading, writing, or reading about writing, Ruthanne enjoys old cartoons with her husband and cats, and dreams of living on an island far, far away.

Find her on: https://youtube.com/ruthannereid | https://patreon.com/ruthannereid/ | https://ruthannereid.com/

www.ingramcontent.com/pod-product-compliance
Lightning Source LLC
Chambersburg PA
CBHW070823170726
48000CB00019B/2419